John Vegiard

The blue and gray: An original allegorical drama of the Civil War of 1861 to 1866

In five acts

John Vegiard

The blue and gray: An original allegorical drama of the Civil War of 1861 to 1866
In five acts

ISBN/EAN: 9783337224516

Printed in Europe, USA, Canada, Australia, Japan

Cover: Foto ©Andreas Hilbeck / pixelio.de

More available books at **www.hansebooks.com**

THE BLUE AND GRAY.

An Original Allegorical Drama of the Civil War of 1861 to 1866.

IN FIVE ACTS.

BY J. T. VEGIARD.

Dedicated to "THE VETERANS."

COSTUMES.

—o—

COL. ST. LEON. Plain gray, or light suit, broad hat, cane.

HARRY PEARSON. Act 1, Scene 1—Riding suit, light. Scene 3—Hunting suit. Act 2—Dark suit, cape. Act 3, Scene 3—Torn shirt and pants, old shoes. Scenes 4 and 5—Gray jacket, slouch hat. Act 4 same as act 2, with head bandaged.

FRANK DUNCAN.—Gray officer's suit, sword &c.

JOHN HARKER. Act 1, Scene 1—Light suit, slouch hat, broad white collar and cuffs, heavy whip. Scene 2—Gray officer's suit, sword &c.

DEITRICK. Act 1—Common overalls. Act 2—Old Union uniform, large front piece on cap, gun. Act 3—Calico dress, Dutch bonnet. Act 4—Same as Act 2.

CHARLES WHITE. Hunting suit; in Act 3, Scenes 3-4—White wig and whiskers, long coat, cane, broad hat.

TEDDY. Act 1—Knee pants, overshirt, old plug hat. Acts 2, 3 and 4—Gray jacket, slouch hat, gun.

ALEX. BURT. Act 1—Rough citizen's dress. Acts 2, 3 and 4—Gray officer's suit, sword, &c.

GENERAL U. S. A. Heavy overcoat, revolver, side arms.

COL. FRANKLIN. Heavy overcoat, revolver, side arms.

GENERAL C. S. A. Full dress Confederate gray, sword, &c.

UNCLE NED. Act 1—Short pants, stockings, shoes, checkered shirt, sleeves rolled up, white curled wig. Act 3—Long coat, old white plug hat.

SAM. Act 1—Livery top boots, &c.

PRISONERS. Old blue uniforms.

SOLDIERS U. S. A. Blue blouses, fatigue caps, light blue pants.

SOLDIERS C. S. A. and GUERRILLAS. Gray suits, slouch hats.

LADIES.

MAUD ST. LEON. Act 1, Scene 1—Riding habit, whip. Scenes 5-6—Light home dress. Act 3—Dark dress, cloak or shawl, hat. Act 4—Brown or dark dress.

MRS. ST. LEON. Act 1—Home dress for old lady, spectacles. Acts 3-4 Dark dress, cloak or shawl, hat.

GODDESS OF LIBERTY. Full Goddess dress.

CAST OF CHARACTERS.

—o—

DEITRICK VONDERSPECK (The Dutch Recruit) ....

COL. ST. LEON (a loyal Southerner) ....

HARRY PEARSON (a Union Spy) ....

FRANK DUNCAN (The Guerrilla Chieftain) ....

JOHN HARKER (St. Leon's Overseer, afterwards a Guerrilla) ....

CHARLES WHITE (Harry's friend, a Union Scout) ....

TEDDY O'CONNOR (a Son of the Old Sod) ....

GENERAL (Com. U. S. Forces) ....

COL. FRANKLIN (of the U. S. Army) ....

UNCLE NED (an Octogenarian) ....

GENERAL (Com. C. S. Forces) ....

SERGEANT (C. S. Army) ....

SAM (one of the Bones of Contention) ....

ALEX. BURT (A Lieutenant of Guerrillas) ....

PRISONER (at Belle Isle) ....

MAUDE ST. LEON (a Loyal Lady, Daughter of St. Leon) ....

MRS. ST. LEON (Wife of the Colonel) ....

RACHE (a Waif) ....

GODDESS OF LIBERTY ....

Officers U. S. A., Officers C. S. A., Citizens, Soldiers, Bushwhackers,
Prisoners, &c., &c.

———

STAGE DIRECTIONS.

———

"R." right. "L." left. "C." center. "L. 1 E." left first entrance. "L.
2 E." left second entrance. "L. U. E." Left upper entrance. "L. C." left
center. "U. C." upper center. "L. H." left hand. "R. 1 E." right first
entrance, &c., &c.

N. B.—"The actor is supposed to be standing on the stage facing the
audience."

THE BLUE AND GRAY.

ACT I.

SCENE 1—Garden or Landscape in 4; Set house L. 3 E.; Set fence from L. to R.; Gate open C., Bench lying R.; Negroes discovered dancing. At conclusion enter UNCLE NED R. 1 E. with garden rake.

UNCLE NED. Git out dar, you good for nuffin niggahs; Clar de grounds. (*All scatter and exit* R. *and* L., *appearing at intervals from behind wings.*) What de goodness you spose dis niggah's gwine to do? Clar de lawn for you common niggahs to dance on! Clar out dar I say, (*leans on rake*). I golly, dem niggahs spose dat I have have got nuffin at all to do but clean up after dem. Taint no use talking. I'm done wid dem; De fust time I ketch um on dis lawn I scrunch dem like a bed bug suah! (*Negroes steal out and commences dancing.* NED *chases them* L. *and* R.) Clar dar, you niggahs; Clar dar I say! (*Enter Harker with whip* L. 1 E.)

HARKER. Get to your work, you black rascals, or I'll skin every one of you. And you Ned, go into the house, the cook may have errands for you to do at the village.

UNCLE NED. (*Bowing*). All right, Massa Harker, and if I ketch any of dem common niggahs round here I'll scrunch em suah.

HARKER. Don't stand around here talking, but go at once. (*Ned exit* L. U. E.) I understand that Frank Duncan has returned to the village, if he has, then I can see him personally and accept his proposition. (*Takes letter from his pocket and reads;*) "HARKER, I hold in my possession a Lieutenancy in the Confederate Army; join me and the position is yours. I will be in the village with my company in a few days. If you can enlist any men do so, and meet me at Munson's store. Yours, FRANK DUNCAN." Ah! here comes the Colonel. (*Enter Col. St. L.*)

COL. ST. L. Well, Harker, how are the farm hands doing this morning?

HARKER. I keep them pretty busy now Colonel; by the by, is there any news stirring?

COL. ST. L. War, War, nothing but war. Ah! what is this? (*Reads*), "*Two men belonging to a notorious band of bushwhackers, commanded by that master cut-throat, Frank Duncan, were hung at Montford last Tuesday.*" So ho! Frank Duncan, instead of entering the Confederate service proper, which would have been bad enough, has turned Guerrilla. And that is the man who wanted my daughter to become his wife. The infernal villain!

HARKER. (*Aside.*) I must get away from here (*looking* R.) excuse me, Colonel, but there are some of those lazy rascals dodging behind the stables (*snapping whip*). Get to your work, you infernal niggers, get to your work. (*Exit* R. 2. E. *Enter Uncle Ned.* L. 1 E.)

UNCLE NED. Oh, Massa Kurnel, I saw dat Massa Duncan down to de village, dressed up in nice grey clothes, wid stars and gold all ober him, and he had such a big cheese knife; golly!

COL. ST. L. Frank Duncan in town; I fear his presence means no good to to the Union men of this vicinity. Thus far we have not been molested; but his presence bodes evil.

UNCLE NED. I golly, Massa Kurnel, here comes de debbil, hisself. (*Ned up stage. Enter Frank Duncan* L. 1 E.)

FRANK D. Ah, St. Leon, how are you to-day. Won't shake hands? No. Well suit yourself. (*Aside*) By and by, St. Leon, you will sing another tune.

COL. ST. L. I am sorry I can't tender you the honors of my house; but to what purpose shall I attribute the honor of this unexpected visit, Mr. Duncan?

FRANK D. (*Aside.*) Mr. Duncan! He used to call me his boy Frank. (*To Col. St. L.*) Colonel, you are not a stranger to the fact that before I entered the Confederate service I loved your daughter and sought her hand from you honorably; you refused to consent to my addresses. Sir, that love has grown stronger and stronger. I now ask you to reconsider the decision you made at my last visit.

COL. ST. L. The decision I then made remains irrevocable. I would never consent that a daughter of mine should marry a man who has basely deserted his country's flag in its hour of dan-

ger. That is not only my decision, but my daughter would
scorn to wed a man who cannot even boast of being an honorable
rebel.

FRANK D. (*Quickly.*) Who dares to say that I am not a true
and honorable soldier?

COL. ST. L. This will explain all, (*reads*); "Two men belonging to a notorious band of bushwhackers, commanded by that
master cut-throat Frank Duncan, were hung at Montford last
Tuesday."

FRANK D. (*Aside.*) Curse those fools, they have betrayed my
secret! Nothing but a bold face will serve me now. (*To Col. St.
L.*) I assure you Colonel it is all a mistake.

COL. ST. L. It is not a mistake (*looks* R), but here comes my
daughter Maude; she shall give the final decision. (*Enter Maude
St. Leon* R. 2 E. *followed by Sam.*)

MAUDE. Father, I had such a splendid ride; Gypsey took me
across the brook by the old mill; thence over the hedge, and——

COL. ST. L. You do not notice that we have company, Maude.

MAUDE. I was not aware. Why Mr. Duncan!

FRANK D. (*Aside.*) Mr. Duncan again. (*To Maude.*) Miss
Maude I had hoped for a better reception after so prolonged an
absence.

COL. ST. L. My child, to save further words, and you and Mr.
Duncan from any embarrassment, I will at once state the object
of his visit. He wishes me to withdraw my former decision in
reference to his suit, and I have, thus far, as I always wish to consult my child's happiness, everything is left in your hands. Are
you willing to marry Frank Duncan?

MAUDE. Father, your decision was mine. Mr. Duncan, I cannot marry a man, however much I might love him, who would
raise his hand in opposition to his country's flag.

COL. ST. L. My own noble girl. Spoken like a St. Leon.

FRANK D. Maude, one word.

MANDE. Mr. Duncan, it is needless to prolong this interview,
and as you have some business of a private nature to transact
with father I may be in the way. Good morning, sir. Follow me
Sam. (*Exit into the house* L. *followed by Sam.*)

FRANK D. (*Aside.*) Yes, ye will have some business of a private
nature to transact, but not at present. (*To Col. St. L.*) Sir, I can

but regret the decision of yourself and daughter, but I shall hope that time may change your views.

Col. St. L. Mr. Duncan, you have heard my decision, which, as I have said before, is irrevocable.

Frank D. Hark you, St. Leon, I have made a decision as irrevocable as yours. Your daughter shall be my wife, though I wade through oceans of blood to obtain her; and if it must be, every house in the township shall be made a beacon light to guide me in my purpose.

Col. St. L. Leave my plantation instantly, sir! You dare to threaten a St. Leon. Leave, sir, or I will order the negroes to assist you.

Frank D. No need of such useless trouble, Col. St. Leon, I will take my leave, (aside), but will soon return. (Exit L. 1 E.)

Uncle Ned. Massa Kurnel, shant I bounce him?

Col. St. L. The infernal scoundrel! To threaten my name with such a dishonor. By jove, I'm sorry I didn't chastise him before he left.

Uncle Ned. Only say de word, Massa Kurnel, and I'll hab de boys ketch him and chuck him into de hoss-pond, and if he says a word I'll scrunch him like a bed-bug, suah.

Col. St. L. Never mind this time, Ned. (Enter Mrs. St. Leon and Maude from house L.)

Mrs. St. L. Colonel, what was the meaning of that loud talking we just heard?

Col. St. L. That insolent traitor, Frank Duncan, has been here, and threatened that If I did not——, but pshaw, no matter. Is dinner near ready?

Maude. Yes, Father, dinner is ready; but we were waiting for Harry, as he has not yet returned from his ride.

Harry. (Outside.) Here, Sam, tell Julius to stable my horse. (Enter L. 2 E.) Ah, aunt, waiting dinner for me, sorry to have kept you. Maude, how do you like your new horse, Gypsey?

Maude. Harry, he is a perfect beauty, and as easy under the saddle as one could wish. You have my thanks for the present; but who do you think has been here this morning?

Harry. I am in the dark; who was it?

Maude. Frank Duncan.

Harry. That accounts for the town being full of cut-throats.

COL. ST. L. I have no doubt they belong to his gang. I fear for the Union men of this vicinity.

MRT. ST. L. Oh, Colonel, I fear the worst. What will become of us all?

HARRY. Become of us? Thank God there are loyal hearts among us who will never shrink from any peril for their country's sake.

MAUDE. I am sure Harry that you will do your best to protect us from this band of assassins. (*Enter Sam from house* L.)

SAM. Massa Kurnel, de dinner am done spoilin.

COL. ST. L. Come Mother, Maude, Harry, let us to our dinner at once. (*Exit into house* L.)

UNCLE NED. I golly, Sam, dar's goin to be a muss suah.

SAM. Gorry mitey! Uncle, is dat so?

UNCLE NED. Dat's what's de matter. But Sam are you goin to fite?

SAM. Me fite? Wha for?

UNCLE NED. For your massa, missus, and de ole plantation.

SAM. Look heah, Uncle, you've seen two dogs fitin ober a bone?

UNCLE NED. Yes.

SAM. Dats de Norf an Souf fitin ober us. Now, Uncle, did you ober see de bone fite? But come long to de kitchen.

UNCLE NED. Hold on, Sam, de ole man's got de rumatics—— Hold on——Hold on. (*Exit* L U E.)

SCENE II.—Landscape in 1.

FRANK D. (*Entering* R 1 E.) So, the doors of the St. Leon mansion are closed against me; little did I think a few hours ago that I should be an outcast from the family where I have always, even from childhood, been received as a friend. My hopes of winning Maud are forever blasted. I will try to forget her. I cannot; her image is firmly implanted in the inmost recessess of my heart. Shall I tamely give her up while my rival, Pearson, curses on him, carries off the prize? No! by all the powers of heaven and earth, she shall be mine! (*Enter Harker* R 1 E.) So, Harker, you received the letter I sent you last week?

HARKER. Yes, Frank, and acting upon your warrant contained therein, I procured this uniform and several men for your band.

FRANK D. Well done, Harker. We will visit the men at once, and our first job will be to ransack and burn the St. Leon mansion, then off to our rendezvous before any of those cursed Yankee scouts happen around this vicinity.

HARKER. I am with you in any scheme against that old aristocrat.

FRANK D. Why! What have you against St. Leon?

HARKER. (Bitterly.) Enough! Has he not treated me more as a servant than as an equal, and when I have punished any of his niggers hasn't he interfered, while his family act as if I was unfit to sit in their presence. I hate them all.

FRANK D. Well, we will make them suffer for our many wrongs. You take some of the notices I have prepared and place them in conspicuous places. I will meet you at Munson's shortly. (Both exit L. 1 E. Enter Uncle Ned R 1 E.)

UNCLE NED. Dar he goes along wid Massar Harker, plotting against my ole Masser Colonel. Well, de ole man must stir his bones and go down to de house. Dese yere are troublesome times an' I fear de colored people of de lan' will hab to stan de brunt. Well, don't stand yere makin' an ole fool ob yerself but git along. (Exit L. 1 E.)

SCENE III.—Plain chamber or Kitchen in 3. Bar L. Tables and chairs R and L. Teddy, Alex Burt and Guerrillas standing near bar.

BURT. Step up, boys, and have a a drink with me. (Guerrillas step to bar.)

TEDDY. Mr. Deitrick, it's a takin of my thrick ye are. Hand thim cards back, ye spalpeen.

DEITRICK. ————dot is goot.

TEDDY. Arrah, now sure the thrick is mine whin yees didn't thrump nor follow suit.

DEITRICK. ————vot vants to cheat me.

TEDDY. Say hare, you stuttering Dutch lunatic, do yese mane to say that Teddy O'Connor was a chate. Badcess to yese for a haythen as doesn't know wan card from anither. (Alex Burt crosses stage.)

BURT. Hello! What's all this disputing about. I'd like to know.

DEITRICK. ————vat I vants of mineself.

TEDDY.   Did yese iver see such a fool at all. Alex?   He thinks we play cards this way—I puts down a card and he takes it, thin he puts down a card and thin I takes it; wan card is as good as anither to him an the jack takes thim all.

DEITRICK.   ————yust vants mine chare.

BURT.   Well, haven't you got your chair?   (Points to Deitrick's chair.)

DEITRICK.   ————und he has more times as me.

BURT.   Oh, I see, you want his dimes—his money.   If I was Teddy I wouldn't give you a picayune.

DEITRICK.   ————yust see like dot now.

BURT.   Ah, yes, I see, he euchred you. didn't he?

DEITRICK.   ———— myself a black eyes.

TEDDY.   Be aff wid ye, be aff.   I want yees to remimber that I have desindid from the Irish Kings.   Me ansister, Roderick O'Connor, was Prince of Connaught, an whin ould Pimbroke was a ravigin Ireland, he was elected King sure; an he fit—till he got licked an thin he gave up, an av yese give me any more of yer blarney I'll put a hid on yese.

DEITRICK.   ————more as two hours lonkar.   (Enter Harker and Guerrilla with bill.)

HARKER.   What do you mean by all this noise?

DEITRICK.   ————my pisness.

HARKER.   Here. Sergeant, stick that bill up there.   (As Sergeant puts up the bill all gather around.)

TEDDY.   (Reading slowly and spelling the words out.)   All a-b-l e, all able, b-o-d-i-e-d, all able bodied min.

DEITRICK.   ————you reats dot of me.

BURT.   (Reading notice.)   "All able bodied men between the ages of twenty and fifty are earnestly called upon to join the Southern Army.   Rally to the call of your countrymen in the field.   One united effort and those Northern hirelings will be driven from our Sunny South."

HARKER.   Come, boys, what will you take to drink?   I am as dry as a fish out of water.   (All step up to the bar and call for drinks.)

DEITRICK.   ————beer ain't you.

TEDDY.   Rather than say yese drink alone, I'll take Irish whisky straight av yese hav it.

HARKER. All right, my man, take something. You will make a good soldier; what do you say, don't you want to join the Southern Army?

TEDDY. Sure an' I'll do that same thing if yese give me good pay and plinty of foightin.

HARKER. We can promise you both, but take another drink. (All turn to bar. Enter Frank Duncan L 1 E.)

FRANK D. Rejected by Maude, who once professed to love me? The one for whom I would sacrifice life itself, with all its pleasures. Driven from the plantation by that old dotard, St. Leon. Curse them, but they will pay dearly for it yet.

HARKER. Have something, Captain?

FRANK D. (To bar.) Yes, give me brandy. I feel as if I could drink an ocean dry, (filling glass, drinks); there I feel better. I was a little out of sorts just now. Deitrick, give us a song?

ALL. A song—a song.

DEITRICK. ————you some dances. (Dances.)

FRANK D. Any more men secured, Harker?

HARKER. I just came in, but Burt has been busy with them.

BURT. They will all go. What do you say my brave fellows?

ALL. Yes! Yes!

FRANK D. Thank you boys, and I'll give each one of you a chance to make a fortune.

BURT. Hurrah for the Captain.

ALL. Hurrah! Hurrah! Hurrah! (Enter Harry and White L 1 E.)

FRANK D. Ah, how are you boys, none in uniform! How is this, Pearson? I thought you would be one of the first to rush to the aid of the unhappy South.

HARRY. I am wanted at home to attend to my old uncle, aunt and cousin, in fact I am a stay at home character.

FRANK D. In place of hiding under petticoats, own up that you have no heart in the Southern cause.

HARRY. Have it your own way, anything to avoid unpleasant argument.

FRANK D. Here, Munson, set up the drinks. Come boys, have something. (Bartender brings five glasses on stand to c; all take glasses but Deitrick.)

DEITRICK. ———drink mineself.

FRANK D. Here's to the health of Jefferson Davis and the Southern Confederacy. Come, Pearson and White, show your colors, don't be afraid.

HARRY. Afraid! No, sir. I am not afraid to say that I despise and detest you and your whole pack of cut-throats just as much as I despise your President, and your would-be Confederacy. I have thus far been neutral, but my heart and sympathies are with the Union now and forever.

WHITE. Bravo! Harry. I am with you.

DEITRICK. ———Ein flag—Ein gountry—Swi lager. (*Drinks.*)

TEDDY. I drinks em both, divil a wan I cares as long as I gets my foightin. (*Drinks.*)

FRANK D. So, Harry Pearson, you follow in the footsteps of your Uncle and take issue with the enemies of the South. Now mark me, I am vested with power from my government to force such as you into our army, and you need not fear but I shall use it.

HARRY. Frank Duncan, you have had your say, now I will have mine. I defy you, or any force you can bring to your aid to force me to raise a hand against the glorious old Stars and Stripes.

FRANK D. You have till dark to make up your minds, then if you are not ready to go willingly force shall be used.

HARRY. Come, White, let us finish our hunt, after to-day we shall have larger game. (*Exit Harry and White L.*)

DEITRICK. ———ven we meets look———(*Frank Duncan starts toward Deitrick, who exits L.*)

FRANK D. Men, to the camp. Harker, take charge till I arrive. (*All exit L 1 E.*) Curse the luck, it has been disappointment after disappointment to-day, but I will yet humble the pride of the St. Leons. First to force that young braggart into our army, and if he refuses to go, shoot him down like a dog. (*Exit L. 1 E.*)

———

SCENE IV.—Landscape in 1. Lights half down. (*Enter Harry, White and Deitrick R 1 E.*)

HARRY. Well here it is evening, and none of us have decided to join the Southern army. I suppose we shall be severely punished for our temerity.

WHITE. I shall not allow the fear of Frank Duncan's wrath to spoil my appetite, and as it is growing late I will bid you good evening; come Deitrick. (*Exit* L. 1 E.)

HARRY. I have had strange foreboding of evil all day upon my mind. At every flash of our guns my Uncle and Frank Duncan would rise before me. What can it mean? But I must shake off these feelings of depression and consider what course to pursue. It will be unsafe for me to remain around here while Frank Duncan and his men are in such close proximity, and I do not relish going into the army either as an officer or private. What else can I do? I have it! I know every part of this State thoroughly and I will tender my services to the Union General to act as spy. I will first consult with my Uncle and if he is willing, go at once. (*Exit* L. 1 E *in haste*.)

SCENE V.—Parlor in 2. Set window R. (*Enter Mrs. St. Leon and Maude* R 1 E.)

MAUDE. I wonder what keeps Harry, he is not usually detained so long while hunting, (*going to window*), I hope nothing has happened.

MRS. ST. L. Do not be impatient child. Harry will, no doubt, be here soon. (*Enter Col. St. L.,* C D.)

MAUDE. Father, I believe Harry wishes to join the Union army; he has spoken to me several times about it of late, but he thought his first duty was with you and mother. (*Enter Harry,* C D.)

COL. ST. L. If it is his wish, I shall make no opposition.

HARRY. Thank you, uncle for those cheering words. Frank Duncan and I had a few sharp words at Munson's store to-day, which resulted in my openly avowing my principles, and he swears that he will either force me into his cut-throat band or shoot me down like a dog.

COL. ST. L. The infernal scoundrel!

HARRY. Uncle, I feel that the time has now arrived for me to join the Union army, and do my share toward putting down this Rebellion.

COL. ST. L. Yes, Harry, your duty points that way; take the best horse in the stable, make your way to the Union camp, and tell the General that old Col. St. Leon has sent you to take his place in the conflict.

MAUDE. Why, Harry, surely you are not going so soon?

HARRY. The sooner the better, Maude; once in the Union lines I can meet Frank Duncan face to face: "I with the Blue, he with the Gray."

MRS. ST. L. Harry, 'tis hard to bid you to leave us, but far be it from me to keep you even one moment from your duty,

MAUDE. My dear cousin, you have our prayers for your success. (*Exit c. d.*)

HARRY. Thank you all for your kind wishes, but I do not go alone. (*Fires revolver through window.*) Do not be alarmed, 'tis but a signal to call my friends. (*Enter Deitrick c. d.*)

DEITRICK. ————to sprecken to der Kurnell.

COL. ST. L. Well, Deitrick, what can I do for you?

DEITRICK. ————dot do dem boorhouse.

COL. ST. L. I will attend to your bequest.

HARRY. We are not going alone, Deitrick, for here comes company. (*Enter White c. d.*)

WHITE. I heard the signal and hastened here at once. What has happened?

HARRY. Nothing of importance, but I have decided to make my way at once to the Union camp, and, wishing company, I called you here. Will you both join me, as I go for one?

WHITE. Count me as two.

DEITRICK. ————dree dimes. (*Mrs. St. Leon goes to window.*)

HARRY. Thank you friends for your decision, but we must make arrangements for our immediate departure.

MRS. ST. L. Harry there must be something unusual going on at Munson's store, as a large crowd has gathered there. (*Enter Maude c. d.*)

MAUDE. Fly Harry! Fly at once, Frank Duncan is coming to force you to join his band.

HARRY. Never fear Maude, he shall not find me unprepared. (*Exit; returns with a rifle, which he places near window.*) There is one good shot at least.

MAUDE. Oh, Harry, fly for my sake, do not, I pray you, tarry here. I hear them even now.

COL. ST. L. Resistance is useless to such numbers, therefore, do not turn our home into a scene of desolation and blood-shed, but fly at once. (*Exit White.*)

HARRY. Uncle, though I detest a skulker and a coward, you shall be obeyed. Farewell Uncle, Aunt, Maude. (*Enter White.*)

WHITE. It is too late, they are making their way across the lawn even now.

MRS. ST. L. May Heaven protect us.

HARRY. (*Looking through window.*) Great heavens! White, your house is one vast sheet of flames.

WHITE. It is indeed so. Frank Duncan has one more item scored against him.

MAUDE. Harry, there is one avenue left; while they are coming up the lawn, you escape through the cellar.

HARRY. Boys, at once to the cellar. (*Exit R. 1 E.*)

DEITRICK. ———der cellar down. (*Exit R. 1 E.*)

COL. ST. L. Thank heaven they are safe! (*Crash heard. Enter Frank Duncan, Harker and Guerrillas, c. D.*)

FRANK D. Caged at last, (*looks around.*) Gone! Old man, where is that sniveling Yankee nephew of yours?

COL. ST. L. Out of your reach, you infernal cut-throat.

FRANK D. 'Tis false! I will have him yet. Search the house from top to bottom; Five hundred dollars for Harry Pearson, dead or alive. (*Exit Harker and Guerrillas, R. and L.*)

COL. ST. L. He has escaped from your clutches, and is safe.

FRANK D. Silence, old man! (*looking through window.*) What is that I see? Harry Pearson making his way across the plantation towards the wood, (*discovers rifle.*) Not so safe as you may think, he has left the means for his own destruction. (*Points rifle through window; Maude snatches revolver from his belt.*)

MAUDE. Fire that rifle at Harry Pearson and my hand will send a bullet through your heart. (*Picture.*) Now he has reached the woods and is safe. (*Drops revolver.*)

FRANK D. (*Sneeringly.*) You shall pay dearly for this at some future time. As I have missed one bird I will make doubly sure of the other. Come along my beauty and do not anger me, by any vain resistance. (*Grasps Maude by the arm.*)

COL. ST. L. (*Raising cane.*) Leave the house or I will chastise you for your insolence.

FRANK D. (*Picking up revolver.*) Chastise me will you? Take that for your insolence. (*Shoots; St. Leon falls; Mrs. St. Leon and Maude kneel by him.*)

MRS. ST. L. Villain! You have murdered my husband!

MAUDE. Wretch! What have you done?

FRANK D. I have but commenced my scheme of vengeance. (*Enter Harker and Guerrillas.*)

HARKER. Smith reports that Union Cavalry is approaching by the east road.

FRANK D. Then we must at once to our saddles; bear that old dotard to the yard. (*Guerrillas exit with St. Leon, C. D.*) As for you, Miss Maude, make all your preparations to become my wife on my return. (*Exit C. D.*)

MAUDE. Come mother, this place is no longer safe for us.

MRS. ST. L. Oh, where shall I go? My husband murdered in cold blood and my nephew driven from home. (*Exit L. 1 E.*)

SCENE VI.—Same as scene 1. Lights down. (Col. St. Leon discovered on Bank R. Enter Mrs. St. Leon from house L. supported by Maude. Cross to R., kneel.

MRS. ST. L. This cross is harder than I can bear. All, all is dark to me. Colonel, husband, may our Father above receive thee.

MAUDE. Mother, mother!

MRS. ST. L. Forgive me, my daughter, if, in grief for the dead, I forget the living. (*Enter Harry L. 1 E.*)

HARRY. Those terrible forebodings are still haunting my mind. I could not leave until I had again beheld my uncle, aunt, and cousin. Why, who are those kneeling there? Tell me, who is that lying there?

MRS. ST. L. Your uncle, who has been murdered.

HARRY. My uncle murdered! (*Kneels in group. Enter Frank Duncan and Harker R. 1 E.*)

FRANK D. Into the house, set fire to it in several places, then escape by the rear. (*Exit; Harker crosses cautiously from R. to L.; exit into house.*)

HARRY. My forebodings are realized, Uncle, dear Uncle, murdered and I not here to protect you. Why are you all so calm? Why do you not weep rivers of tears? See those white locks dyed with the life current from his gaping wounds. Who did this terrible deed?

Mrs. St. L.   Frank Duncán.

Harry.   Frank Duncan's image came into my mind with my uncle's as if some terrible link connected them together. You see I am calm, tell me all.

Maude.   After you had gained the wood, Frank Duncan, enraged at your escape, rudely grasped my arm, and tried to drag me from the room; father, seizing his cane, sought to protect me, when Frank Duncan shot him down in rold clood and fled immediately, hotly pursued by the Union Cavalry who heard the firing.

Harry.   Gone!   Escaped! and I not nigh to avenge the wrong. Oh, why were the thunderbolts of Heaven silent when such a bloody deed was done. (*Fires pistol ; enter White* L. 1 E.) Hold, White, ask no questions until I have told you all—a story that will make the blood curdle in your veins: There lies my uncle, murdered by that fiend in human shape, Frank Duncan. (*Fire seen in house* L.) What is that, our house in flames; let us save what we can. (*As the door is opened flames burst out.*) Too late! too late! Aunt, Maude, pray for us. (*Draws revolver and kneels.*) Our mission is revenge.

(*Tableau—Curtain.*)

◆ ◆ ◆

ACT II.

SCENE I.—Log house or kitchen in 4. Set door R. 2 E. Set fire place L. 2 E. Bed against flat c. Table and stools L. Lights half down. (Deitrick discovered in bed with curtains closed.) Rain heard, lightning and thunder at intervals.

Deitrick.   ————mean puy sudch conduct like dose. (*Knock heard ; Deitrick crosses to door.*) ————de inside oud?

Harry.   It is me, Harry.

Deitrick.   ————myself pack yet, aind id? (*Opens door; enter Harry.*)

Harry.   'Tis a terrible night out, where is White?

Deitrick.   ————rains like de tuyval.

Harry.   Fix up a little, Deitrick, I expect company. (*Sits* L. *leans head on table.*)

Deitrick.   ————as my name is Deitrick.

Harry.   Revenge! (*Strikes hand on table; startles Deitrick.*)

DEITRICK. ————dot so!

HARRY. The night Frank Duncan killed my uncle and burned our house, I swore an oath of vengeance; as a spy I gain access into the rebel lines; four of his band have fallen by my hand and he shall soon follow them. I expect some Union officers, to whom I shall impart information of importance.

DEITRICK. ————a uniforms like dot?

HARRY. Here we live secluded, no one knows our intentions, except those I expect; should I wear a uniform of blue I could not gain admittance into the rebel lines. (*Knocks at door* R.) Ah! that is the signal, open the door Deitrick. (*Deitrick unfastens door, enter* General U. S. A., Colonel Franklin and Officer.) Welcome, gentlemen, I am glad to meet you.

GENERAL. We thank you for your greeting, but who have I the pleasure of addressing?

HARRY. Harry Pearson, known to your army as "The Avenger."

GENERAL. Harry Pearson! Can you be the son of my old classmate at West Point, Col. Pearson. the hero of Vera Cruz, and nephew of Colonel St. Leon?

HARRY. The same.

GENERAL. Where is your uncle?

HARRY. Dead, foully murdered, and that is why I, in place of joining your ranks, lead the roving life of a spy. But time is flying, General, here are some important dispatches I captured from one of the enemy's couriers. They will attack your camp early to-morrow morning in overwhelming numbers, intending to capture the pickets and take you by surprise.

GENERAL. Then we will be prepared to receive them. Many thanks till I can reward your valuable services better. Join our ranks and I will see that you receive a commission, and it will be safer, as I understand there is a heavy reward offered for you, dead or alive.

HARRY. General, do not try to tempt me from fulfilling my oath. I will willingly impart to you any information which I can obtain, but now I only live for revenge.

GENERAL. Gentlemen, let us at once to our camp. Pearson, whenever you may wish to see me, send word by the same messenger as before. Adieu. (*Harry opens door.*)

HARRY. Adieu General, you shall soon hear from me again.

(*Closing door.*) 'Tis clearing up, the worse for my undertaking.

DEITRICK. (*Trying to put on shoe.*) ———efer gets dot poots on.

WHITE. (*Outside* R.) I say, Deitrick, open the door.

HARRY. Ah! White, I will open the door for him.

DEITRICK. ———him sure. (*Harry opens door; enter White conducting Burt.*)

HARRY. Who have you there, White? A Confederate officer, as I live.

WHITE. He strayed a little too close to our retreat, so we captured him and brought him in. We did not know but you could use him for some purpose.

HARRY. You were right, I need a Confederate uniform, and at once.

BURT. Sir, as an officer in the Southern army, and captured in uniform, I demand that you treat me as a prisoner of war and a gentleman.

DEITRICK. ———you dot vay.

HARRY. We shall treat you as a gentleman and a soldier, but it is necessary that I have your coat and hat for a few hours.

BURT. I protest against your taking either, sir.

HARRY. Then we shall be obliged to take them by force, much as I may regret the necessity.

DEITRICK. ———mat, I tole you dot.

BURT. Rather than submit to personal violence, I give them up, but under protest. (*Takes off coat and hat.*)

HARRY. Are you not the bearer of dispatches?

BURT. I refuse to answer, (*glancing quickly at right boot.*)

HARRY. I will trouble you to take off yur right boot.

DEITRICK. ———it off. (*White holds Burt; Deitrick pulls off boot and rolls over; papers fall out.*) ———somedings by jibbity. (*Rubbing himself.*)

HARRY. (*Picking up papers.*) The very thing. With these papers I can make my way to headquarters. (*Putting on Burt's coat and hat and whiskers from box on table.*) I am going inside the Confederate lines. Guard your prisoner well, as upon your vigilance depends my safety. (*Deitrick lets him out of door.*)

WHITE. We will have to compel you to stay here until the Captain returns; so make yourself as comfortable as possible; only remember, the first effort you make to escape will be met by a closer confinement.

DEITRICK. ————look oud vonce.

BURT.   I will try to get a little sleep, if you have a spare blanket.

WHITE. (*Getting blankets* L.) There, make yourself at home, (*yawns*). I guess I am a little sleepy, too. Deitrick, you stand guard for a couple of hours, then I will relieve you. Why, how sleepy I am (*yawns.*) Well, I'll turn in. (*Take blankets and lie down before fire* L.)

DEITRICK. ————, but dot aind so. (*Goes to sleep; Burt rises cautiously, crosses to door.*)

BURT.   Sleep on, my Teutonic friend, your drowsiness has proved my salvation. (*Exit* R.)

DEITRICK. ————, he done escaped himself oud. (*White jumps up, grasps gun.*)

WHITE.   The prisoner gone! How did he escape?

DEITRICK. ————no vere I seed him.

WHITE.   Most likely you was asleep.

DEITRICK. ————vasn't asleep.

WHITE.   Come Deitrick, we must re-capture that rebel, or Harry is lost! (*White exits through door* R.)

DEITRICK. (*Putting on overcoat.*) ————so help me gimminy jinglewax. (*Exit* R.)

————

SCENE II. –Landscape in 2. (Enter Teddy L. 2 E., on guard.

TEDDY.   I wish this tarnation war was inded. It is nothing but foight and stand on guard all the time, (*yawns.*) I haven't had a dacent night's rest for a week, and they have given us orders to be extramely watchful to-night. Halt! who comes there? (*Looks* R.)

HARRY. (*Outside.*) A friend.

TEDDY.   Advance and give the countersign. (*Enter Harry* R. 2 E.)

HARRY.   I have dispatches of the utmost importance and must see the General at once.

TEDDY.   I will sind for the Officer of the Gaard, (*look* L.) Most likely this is the General approaching, he sometimes comes around the outposts. Halt! who comes there?

HARKER. (*Outside.*) Grand Rounds.

TEDDY. Advance, Sergeant of Grand Rounds, and give the countersign. (*Enter Sergeant of Rebels, gives countersign.*) Countersign correct, pass rounds. (*Exit to place. As Grand Rounds enter* L. *Teddy steps forward, salutes Harker.*) Officer of the Guard, this officer here says he has dispatches of importance for the General, (*resumes station.*)

GENERAL. Well sir, what papers have you?

HARRY. (*Producing dispatches.*) General, these dispatches were handed me by Major St. Clair, who has been severely wounded, and he requested me to deliver them to you, in person.

GENERAL. Thanks, but to whom am I indebted for their safe delivery? (*Harker, who has been closely watching Harry, draws revolver.*

HARKER. Do not attempt to escape!

GENERAL. What means this outrage, Lieutenant?

HARKER. (*Pulling off Harry's whiskers.*) General, allow me to introduce Harry Pearson, the Union Spy, more properly known as "The Avenger." (*Harry folds his arms.*)

GENERAL. Ha! Then you are the man we are ordered to keep a close watch for. What infernal scheme have you on hand now that brings you into our lines?

HARRY. I refuse to answer any questions.

FRANK D. (*Entering* L. 1 E.) General, I just heard of your intended surprise of the Union camp to-morrow morning, and I come to volunteer the services of my band. What! Pearson. Ha! Ha! my fine bird, caged at last.

GENERAL. You know him Duncan, who is he?

HARRY. The avenger of my uncle's murder. (*Grasps Frank Duncan by the throat.*)

GENERAL. Secure him guards. (*Teddy and Guerrilla seize Harry.*) Young man, your case is desperate; I have orders to shoot you as soon as captured.

HARRY. Such is generally the custom of Guerrillas, but hark you, General, it is life for life, a "Gray for a Blue."

GENERAL. I do not take your meaning.

HARRY.   But a few miles from here your courier is a prisoner; if I do not return my men will hang him to the first tree. (*Enter Burt* R. 1 E.)

BURT.   General, I was captured by a party of scouts but a short distance from here (*points to Harry*), and there stands their leader. I'll trouble you for my coat and hat.

HARRY.   Now my fate is sealed. (*Takes off coat and hat, hands them to Burt.*)

GENERAL.   (*Shaking hands with Burt.*)   Allow me to congratulate you. And now, I shall not hesitate to mete out to you the penalty prescribed by my superior.

FRANK D.   General, there is a little matter of long standing between the prisoner and myself, and if my well-known services would entitle me to the privilege of carrying out his sentence, you can call on me for any favor in return.

GENERAL.   Your request shall be granted. Captain Duncan, you will see that my orders are strictly carried out, and these soldiers will be under your command until I receive your report. Come, Lieutenant and Sergeant, let us at once to our quarters. (*Exit General and staff* L. 2 E.)

FRANK D.   Harry Pearson, you are at last in my power. Prepare for the journey which you are about to take into a new country.

HARRY.   When I first undertook the hazardous life of a spy, I made all my preparations to meet death face to face; but I warn you, Frank Duncan, by murdering me, you will not escape your just doom, for others are on your path who will execute the oath I swore against the murderer of my aged uncle.

FRANK D.   No more. I will hear no more. Teddy place him yonder. (*Teddy places Harry* R. 2 E.) Now men——ready——aim——(*Shots heard* R. *Exit Frank Duncan, Teddy and Guerrillas* L. 2 E. *in haste. Enter White and Deitrick* R. 2 E. *White hands Harry a gun.*)

WHITE.   Take this gun; we must at once gain the protection of our cabin, or all will be taken.

HARRY.   Thanks, White, but let us start at once. That was a close shave for me. (*Exit Harry and White* R.)

DEITRICK.   ————tuyval, aind id. (*Looks around, seeing the rest have gone, exits hastily* R. *Enter Frank Duncan and Guerrillas* L. 2 E.)

FRANK D. Escaped! Follow me at once in their path; take them, dead or alive! (*Guerrillas exit* R. *Enter Harker, Burt, General and staff* L. 2 E.) General, the spy has escaped, rescued by his friends, who have killed our pickets.

GENERAL. Escaped! Have you ordered out an attachment in pursuit?

FRANK D. Yes, General, at once.

GENERAL. Follow them yourself: leave not a stone unturned to effect his re-capture; then take him, if alive, to Belle Isle—let him starve for his audacity. (*Exit Frank Duncan* R. 2 E.) Gentlemen, let us at once to the attack—all now depends upon quick actions. To your saddles immediately—ride for your lives. One hour in the field is worth a whole day here.

(*All exit* L. 2 E.)

———

SCENE III.—Wood in 1. Rain heard. (Enter Harry, White and Deitrick L. in haste.

HARRY. At last we are free from those human blood-hounds.

WHITE. Yes, we have thrown them off the scent; let us at once to our retreat; gather whatever we wish to take with us, and abandon this section for a time at least.

HARRY. You are right, since Burt knows of its whereabouts, the place will be made too hot to hold us. Deitrick, you stand guard here, while we get ready for a start. Can you keep your eyes open now?

DEITRICK. ——— —— myself of him—dot's so.

HARRY. Come, White, let us hasten. (*Exit* R. *followed by White.*)

DEITRICK. ———graves, mit sorrows. (*Enter Teddy* L. *in haste.*) ———who vas you?

TEDDY. Don't yese remimber me, Deitrick?—Teddy O'Connor.

DEITRICK. ———, I guess not!

TEDDY Will, I am sorry for any misunderstandin' we hed, sure, an' I axes yere pardin.

DEITRICK. ———mark dime—March. (*Aims gun, Teddy attempts to put his hands in his pockets.*)

DEDDY. Ye dirty spalpeen ye, but——

DEITRICK. ———no nonsendees. (*Enter Frank Duncan* L.)

Stob quick—trow up your hants—mark dime—or I kills myself. (*Frank Duncan marks time.*)

FRANK D.   You infernal Dutchman, I'll——

DEITRICK.   ————shendlemens on guard. (*Enter Guerrilla* L.) ————der gourt knows herself. (*Enter two Guerrillas,*) ————keep id ub, or I vires. (*Enter Harker,* R. *Creeps cautiously toward Deitrick.*) ————sdardt a graveyarts—vall in—(*Harker pinions Deitrick's arms, Frank Duncan places handkerchief over his mouth; Teddy grasps his gun.*)

TEDDY.   There, ye dirty spalpeen. Ye wouldn't shake hands wid Teddy O Connor——

FRANK D.   Silence fool! Do you want to alarm our game? Take him along with us. (*Guerrillas pick up Deitrick.*)

HARKER.   Now, Captain, our birds are once more within our reach.

(*All exit* R.)

———————

SCENE IV.—Same as scene 1, Same Act. (Enter General U. S. A., Colonel Franklin, and two officers R.)

GENERAL.   Pearson not here. What could have become of him?

COL. FRANKLIN.   Most likely he has gone on one of his many expeditions, and will return ere long.

GENERAL.   I fear for his safety. Since learning that he whom we knew so long as "The Avenger," was the son of my old friend, Col. Pearson, I have taken a great interest in his welfare.

COL. FRANKLIN.   I hear footsteps, General: you are imperiling your safety by remaining so long outside our lines.

GENERAL.   No man, who is an honorable soldier, whether General or Private, should be afraid to meet death in any form or shape.

COL. FRANKLIN.   The footsteps are approaching this way; let us sell our lives dearly if they are enemies. (*Draws Revolver.*)

(*Enter Harry and White* R.)

GENERAL.   Ah! returned—I had fears for your safety.

HARRY.   This has been an eventful night to me, General. After you left here I returned to the Confederate camp in disguise, was discovered, and about to be shot, when my brave friends rescued me. Our retreat is known, and as Frank Duncan's guerrillas were in full chase after us, you had better leave at once, and I will shortly follow you.

GENERAL. Again you have placed me under obligations to you. To-morrow I wish you near me if there is a battle to be fought. Will you not accept a position on my staff?

HARRY. Yes, but for the day only. This is my place until I have fully avenged all wrongs. But, General, fly ere it be too late. (*Exit General U. S. A., Col. Franklin and Officers. Harry casts himself on bed.*)

HARRY. Again those terrible forebodings of evil come before my mind. What do they foretell? Can they mean danger to my aunt and cousin? Oh my poor unhappy South, why did you bring this righteous judgment upon you?

WHITE. Come, Harry, we have not much time to lose (*noise heard in the distance* R.) Hark! There is some one approaching. (*Harry jumps from bed, opens door. Shot heard.*)

HARRY. (*Closing door.*) That was a narrow escape. We will have to make a stand here, as it is too late for flight.

WHITE. They must have either killed or captured Deitrick, though I did not hear a shot fired.

HARKER. (*Outside.*) Surrender and your lives will be spared; resist and we will burn the house.

HARRY. (*Shooting through window.*) Take that for your answer. (*Shots heard outside; suddenly all is still.*)

WHITE. What can they be doing?

HARRY. They are gathering brush to fire the house. We must escape by the secret passage; you go while I keep them at bay. (*Fires lit.*)

WHITE. 'Tis you they want, let me stay.

HARRY. There is no time for argument, go at once. (*Exit White through trap. Door bursts open, enter Guerrillas. Harry fires, one falls. Enter Frank Duncan and Harker, who grasps Harry as he enters trap.*)

FRANK D. Ah, my bird, caught again. This time you go to Belle Isle.

(*Tableau—Curtain.*)

ACT III.

Here a Battle Scene may be introduced, when wanted, with Marches, Drills, Evolutions, &c.

J. T. VEGIARD.

ACT IV.

SCENE I.—Same as Act 1, Scene 1. (Uncle Ned and Negroes discovered.)

UNCLE NED. Help de old man up on de bench, he wants to tole you something. (*All help Ned on the bench.*) Now, you common niggahs, listen to what I tole yer: Missus says dat yer are all free. (*All shout.*) Dat you 'ken go when you please, and whar yer please widout any Masser or Missus. (*Shout.*) Masser Lincum dun sign de mancipashun proclamashun, so dat now yuse as good as de white folks. (*Shout.*) So all dose dat wants to work for demselves, pack up deir duds and bid good-bye to Missus. (*All exit* L. *but Uncle Ned and Sam.*)

SAM. Uncle Ned, what is you gwine to do?

UNCLE NED. Sam. I was born on dis plantation, an when Masser St. Leon was a little boy I toted him around, an now dat he is dead an gone, does ye spose I am gwine to go away an leab de ole Missus?

SAM. Look a heah Uncle Ned, you is as good as de white folks; now why doesn't you join de Bobolishun party and run for Congress?

UNCLE NED. You can do dat Sam, as for me, I'll stick by de ole plantation.

SAM. Well, good-bye Uncle, dis chile is gwine suah.

UNCLE NED. Good-bye Sam, and when you gits to Congress don't forget yer old Uncle. (*Exit Sam* L.) Taint no use talkin, dem darkies 'ull wish dey was back on de ole plantation fore long. (*Enter Mrs. St. Leon and Maude* L. U E.)

MRS. ST. L. How well our old home has been made to look.

MAUDE. Yes, mother, it was a miracle that naught but the kitchens and upper chambers were destroyed.

UNCLE NED (*bowing*.) Beg pardon, Missus, but de ole house looks kind of natural.

MRS. ST. L. Yes, Uncle, just as natural as of old; but did you instruct the hands that they were now free to go where they please?

UNCLE NED. Yes, Missus, an heah dey cum. (*Negroes cross* L. *to* R. *with bundles.*)

NEGROES. Good-bye, Missus.

MRS. ST. L. Farewell—a kind farewell to all.

MAUDE. How sad one feels to even part from a servant.

MRS. ST. L. Good-bye, Uncle Ned, 'tis with the deepest regret I part with you.

UNCLE NED. Missus, I isn't a gwine. I was born on dis plantation, and wid your leab I'll die heah. I'se old now, Missus, an' can't do much; but what I can do I will do. You won't send me away, Missus?

MRS. ST. L. No, Uncle Ned, while I have a roof over my head you shall share it with me.

UNCLE NED. Tank you, Missus, tank you; any place is good enough for me.

MAUDE. If Harry was only here to enjoy this, our return to the old homestead.

MRS. ST. L. I fear, Maude, for his safety; 'tis over six months since we have heard aught of him. (*Enter Deitrick* R. U. E. *in haste.*)

DEITRICK. ————vich vay I gone.

MAUDE. Go into the house; there you will find some old clothes with which you can disguise yourself. (*Exit Deitrick into house* L.) Mother, we must detain his pursuers at all hazards. Uncle Ned, you run down the lawn, and throw them off the track if you can.

UNCLE NED. I'se gwine, Miss Maude, an' if dey insist on cummin, I'll scrunch dem like a bed-bug. (*Exit* R. U. E.)

MRS. ST. L. God grant we can save him from those terrible men·

MAUDE. If they belong to Frank Duncan's guerrillas, they are as bloodthirsty as their master.

MRS. ST. L. 'Tis strange that Frank has not troubled us since the fire.

MAUDE. He knows my feelings, and perhaps has foregone his determination to force me to become his wife.

UNCLE NED (*outside.*) I tell you, Masser Harker, dat dey haint nobody cum dis way, suah.

HARKER (*outside.*) Stand aside, you black rascal!—I'll see for myself. (*Enter Harker and two Guerrillas* R. U. E., *followed by Uncle Ned.*) Ah, ladies, excuse me.

MAUDE. John Harker, what means this outrage? I think that you and your villainous master have injured our family enough, without putting us to further trouble.

MRS. ST. L. Leave this plantation at once, or I will make a complaint to your superiors.

HARKER (*bowing.*) My superiors would pay but little attention to one that bears the reputation of being the aunt of a Union Spy. I am sorry to trouble you, Mrs. St. Leon, but a prisoner has escaped from us, and we have traced him here.

MRS. ST. L. I assure you that you will not find him inside of my house, but, Mr. Harker, can you tell me any news concerning my nephew, Harry?

HARKER (*aside.*) Here is the opportunity to throw in a word for Frank Duncan. Yes, madam, six moths ago Harry Pearson was captured by the Confederate forces, and condemned to be hung as a spy; through the intercession of Frank Duncan, he was reprieved, and is now in prison at Belle Isle.

MAUDE. Then Frank Duncan had some other of his villainous schemes in view. Perhaps he is being slowly starved to death, like many of our poor boys in blue.

HARKER. We are losing time in parleying thus. Men, search the house!

MAUDE. Hold! You enter that house at your peril (*draws revolver, takes position* C.) If your master is rowdy enough to take advantage of two unprotected females, then I am woman enough to defy you all. (*Picture.*)

HARKER. Stand aside, or will order my men to fire.

MAUDE. Coward, do you fear one woman? You can enter the house, but you will not find a single soul within. (*Aside.*) Ere this he has escaped by the rear door.

HARKER. Search the house from top to bottom. (*Guerrillas exit into house.*) If he is found within, rest assured your conduct will be reported to our Commanding General.

Mrs. St. L. We will abide the issue. (*Enter Deitrick* L. 1. E *disguised as a female.*)

Deitrick. ——————laties of dot houses?

Mrs. St. L. Yes; what can we do for you?

Deitrick ——————I bin Deitrick.

Maude. What can you do, my good woman?

Deitrick. ——————on der laties.

Mrs. St. L. I think we shall need your services, as all of our help are gone.

Deitrick. ——————has got von like dot.

Harker. Did any one pass you as you were coming across the plantation?

Deitrick. ——————you tole me.

Harker. Did you see a man as you came along?

Deitrick. ——————mans?

Harker. Yes, a man.

Deitrick. ——————gap like dot way?

Harker. Yes! yes!

Deitrick. ——————Somepody like dot.

Harker. Curse you for a stupid Dutch fool. (*Exit into house* L.)

Deitrick. ——————dond I vools him?

Maude. Be quiet; if he should suspect your trick, all is lost. (*Enter Harker and Guerrilllas from house.*)

Harker. He is not in the house. Come, men, this way. (*Exit* L. 1 E.)

Mrs. St. L. Thank heaven, he has gone.

Deitrick. ——————for der situvations.

Maude. Hasten into the house—they may return.

Deitrick. ——————afder Misdur Harry.

Mrs. St. L. Do you think he can be freed, Deitrick?

Deitrick. ——————name is Deitrick. (*Exits into house* L.)

Mrs. St. L. Come into the house; there we can arrange some means to send him relief. (*Both exit into house* L.)

SCENE II.—*Landscape in 1.* (*Enter* White L.)

WHITE.   I can gain no information of Harry's whereabouts. Twice have I been inside the Confederate lines, and returned disappointed. (*Looks* R.)   Who is that coming this way?—a woman, as I live. (*Enter Deitrick* R. *courtesies.*)

DEITRICK.   (*aside.*) ————do dot villages.

WHITE.   Yes, my good woman, but are you not afraid to be so near the rebel lines, and alone?

DEITRICK.   ————dot repel vellars.

WHITE.   Come along, I will show you the way.

DEITRICK.   ————ashamet of you.

WHITE.   What—Deitrick?

DEITRICK.   ————my goot vomans.

WHITE.   Why, I heard that you had been captured.

DEITRICK.   ————I valked off.

WHITE.   Well, I am glad you escaped, but what means this disguise?

DEITRICK.   ————geds him oud.

WHITE.   Harry a prisoner at Belle Isle;—then I will disguise myself as an old man and go with you. Meet me near the ruins of our old cabin. (*Exit* R.)

DEITRICK.   ————free of dot brisons out. (*Enter Harker* L.)

HARKER.   Confound that Dutchman, how he fooled me. Ah! that Dutch woman I saw at St. Leon's.

DEITRICK   ————do, Misdur? (*Courtesies.*)

HARKER.   Do you know that I think you are not such a fool as you look?

DEITRICK.   ————dot so?

HARKER.   And come to look, you resemble that Dutch prisoner I had this morning.

DEITRICK.   ————got oud of dis blaces.

HARKER.   Yes, and I will have to search you before you leave here.

DEITRICK.   ————in dis vide vorlt.

HARKER   Alone or not, I am determined to search you. (*As*

Harker grasps his left hand, Deitrick draws revolver and knocks him down.)

DEITRICK.   ————in bettigoats? (*Exit* R.)

HARKER. (*Rising up slowly.*) Curse that infernal she devil! though I believe it was that Dutchman in disguise. How heavy my head feels; I will find my men, then pursue and capture him. (*Staggers out* L.)

————

SCENE III.—Stockade or prison in 3; lights half down. (Harry and Union prisoners discovered lying on stage L. Rebel guard on stockade.) TABLEAU—"The Prisoner's Dream of Home."

HARRY. Oh God, will these inhuman fiends ever bring me anything to eat? (*Raising up.*) For thirty-six hours not even a crumb has passed my lips. Can Frank Duncan mean to keep that fearful oath he swore when I was first incarcerated in this horrible den. Does he think he can starve me into acquiescence to his wishes? Though naught but a ghastly skeleton were left of my once strong frame, I would still bid him defiance. The hope of once more seeing my poor aunt and cousin is all that sustains me now. (*Enter Frank Duncan* R. 1 E. *with guards.*

FRANK D. Ah, good evening, Harry Pearson, your rations do not agree with you, if I should judge by your present condition.

HARRY. Do you come to mock my sufferings, inhuman fiend that you are?

FRANK D. I come as a friend, to bring you this, my last offer.

HARRY. Speak, man, what would you say?

FRANK D. I am in full command of this prison at the present time: here you are slowly but surely starving. Not many weeks will elapse ere you will sink into your grave, unknown and uncared for. I offer you life and liberty. Leave the Northern army—join us; tell Maude that you owe all to me, and rank and riches shall be yours. Refuse me and your torture shall be tenfold.

HARRY. I do refuse you, and with scorn. You offer me life and liberty, the two greatest boons to an American heart—but at what a price? My manhood. I warn you, Frank Duncan, should you fulfill your threat and kill me, my spirit would haunt you till your dying day, the same as my poor murdered uncle's does at the present.

FRANK D. (*Aside, looking hastily around.*) What can he mean? Does he, too, see that old man, with gory locks and haggard face, that is forever glaring at me with his ghastly eyes? No—pshaw! Why do I conjure up such fancies. (*To Harry.*) Harry Pearson, beware how you refuse this, my last offer.

HARRY. Though death stood ready to claim me instantly, my answer would remain the same.

FRANK D. Then starve and rot here, you infernal Yankee spy; as for Maude, I will tear her from her home at once, and if she refuses to become my wife, I will make her beg, at my feet for the position.

HARRY. Inhuman fiend! but go—leave me.

FRANK D. I leave you now, but remember that Frank Duncan always keeps his oath. (*Exit* R.)

HARRY. Heaven is now my only hope—I will not repine, but try to say "Thy will, not mine, be done."

PRISONER. Will they ever bring us food?

HARRY. Do not be down-hearted, comrade; when all earthly hope forsakes you, look to heaven for guidance. (*Enter Frank Duncan*, R. 1 E.)

FRANK D. Guards, be extremely vigilant; shoot the first pris-oner that crosses the dead-line. Thirty day's furlough for a dead Yank. (*Enter Deitrick and White* R. *in disguise, followed by guard with lantern.*) Here are the prisoners; look around, and see if you can find the one you are in search of.

DEITRICK. ———————— mit all dese brisoners.

HARRY. (*Aside.*) Deitrick here—what can all this mean?

DEITRICK. (*Getting between White and Frank D. White passes revolver to Harry.*) ———————dill ve finds him.

FRANK D. How did you say the mistake happened?

DEITRICK. ————————vas but in der brisons.

FRANK D. Well, let us find him if he is here, and your request for his release shall be granted.

DEITRICK. (*Speaking loud.*) ———————— do vind boor Deitrick. (*White nods his head. All exit* L. 2 E.)

HARRY. Hope again springs to my heart; with this weapon I can, at least, take life for life. (*Lies down. Enter Teddy* R. 2. E. *cautiously.*)

TEDDY. Begorra, there goes that murderin' spalpeen, Captain Frank Duncan, so that I'll have at laste a minit to look for Mister Harry Pearson.

HARRY. Who speaks my name?

TEDDY. Phwist, ye divil. An' sure are yese Mister Harry Pearson?

HARRY. That is my name, but who are you?

TEDDY. Sure me name is Teddy O'Connor. Don't yese remimber the time that I came to your uncle's place, nothin but a skileton; an' sure didn't ye, like a big-hearted fellow as ye are, take me into the kitchen, and give me plinty to ate an' dhrink.

HARRY. Are you the one?

TEDDY. Yis; an' fearin' yese might be hungry, sure I brot ye a loaf of bread.

HARRY. (*Grasping bread.*) Thank you, my brave fellow, and be assured that Teddy O'Connor will never be forgotten by me.

TEDDY. Here's a ribil uniform for ye, (*pulls off jacket and hat.*) The countersign is "BEAUREGARD." Bad luck to him, it ought to be Blackguard.

HARRY. "Cast thy bread upon the waters, for it will return ere many days."

TEDDY. Throw it into the wather, is it? Throw nice swate aitin bread into the wather? Begorra, I wouldn't gev it to ye if I thought ye was goin' to throw it in the water. I'd better make myself scarce, as here comes Frank Duncan. (*Exit R. in haste. Enter Frank Duncan, Deitrick, White and guard L. Harry conceals bread.*)

FRANK D. Then he is not here?

DEITRICK. ————Dond gan vind him.

FRANK D. Dry your eyes, my good woman, you may be more fortunate at Libby Prison.

DEITRICK. ————a boor vomans.

FRANK D. I can never do too much for a loyal Southerner. Come to my office and I will give you a pass that will take you any place inside our lines.

DEITRICK. ————god der basses. (*All exit R.*)

HARRY. Here, comrades, I have a loaf of bread. (*All crowd to F. C. Harry divides bread. In going back, prisoner steps over dead-line. Guard shoots him, and others drag him back.*)

ALL.   Shame! shame! (*All exit slowly* L.)

HARRY.   Another martyr to liberty!—but morning is approaching—I must hasten to leave this infamous den. (*Puts on rebel
coat and hat.*)

PROMPTOR. (*Outside* R.)   Halt! Who comes there?

HARRY. (*Outside.*)   A friend.

PROMPTOR.   Advance, and give the countersign.—Countersign
correct. (*Exit Harry* R. 1 E. *Enter Frank Duncan* R. 1 E. *with
guards.*)

FRANK D.   Once more to gloat over the sufferings of Harry Pearson, then visit Maude, and force her to become my wife. (*Looks
around.(* Not here! Why 'twas but a moment ago I saw him in
this very place. Come to think, who was that Confederate soldier
who passed us at the gate? Curses on him—he has escaped.
Sound the alarm at once! Let loose the blood-hounds! hunt him
to death. *Frank Duncan and Guerrillas exit* R. 2. E. in haste.)

SCENE IV.—*Landscape in 1.*   (*Enter Deitrick and White* L.)

DEITRICK.   ————wigs on, aind id. (*Noise heard* L.)

WHITE.   Yes; but what means that noise at the prison. Can
they suspect us?

DEITRICK.   ————hobe nod. (*Enter Harry* L. *in haste.*)

HARRY.   Ah, friends, I have just escaped from that infernal
prison.

DEITRICK.   ————pack py jibbity.

WHITE.   Strike at once for the swamps, and we will try to throw
your pursuers from the trail. (*Exit Harry* R. *in haste.*)

DEITRICK.   ————my dwo eyes yet. (*Enter Frank Duncan,
Alex. Burt, and Guerrillas* L.)

FRANK D.   Did you see a man dressed as a Confederate soldier
pass along this road?

DEITRICK.   ————mid der hibelwirken.

FRAND D.   I want none of your infernal Dutch lingo, but plain
English.

DEITRICK.   ————seen any podies.

FRANK D.   Come on, men, at once for the blood-hounds, they
will find his trail. (*Exit* R. *with guards.*)

DEITRICK. — ———like my dresses.

WHITE. Very good, Deitrick, but you are not in style.

DEITRICK. ————in der styles.

WHITE. Why you haven't any pin back.

DEITRICK. ————Frank Duncan catches Harry.

WHITE. (*Pulling Deitrick's arm.*) Come along, hurry up. (*Exit* R.

———

SCENE V.—Rocky pass in 4. Stream c. Set log R. Set rocks R. 3 E. Enter Harry L. 1 E. Falls.

HARRY. Hark! I hear the baying of those terrible bloodhounds —'tis too late for further flight. There are seven charges in this revolver—six for them and one for myself before I will be re-taken. (*Fires* L.) One less. (*Fires.*) Missed! (*Fires.*) Both dead, and four charges left—these I will reserve for human bloodhounds. Now for the stream. (*Exit* R. 1 E. *Enter Frank Duncan, Burt, and guard,* L. 1 E. *Harry appears on log* R.)

FRANK D. Just in time—die—(*Harry fires—one guard fails. Frank Duncan fires—Harry reels.*)

HARRY. Oh, heavens! I am shot. Frank Duncan, may my curse haunt you—(*Falls into stream.*)

FRANK D. Let us leave this place. That curse will ring in my ears forever. (*Frank Duncan and guards exit* L. *in haste. Enter Deitrick, who draws Harry from stream.*)

DEITRICK. Ish dot so!

(*Tableau—Curtain.*)

———◆◆◆———

ACT V.

SCENE I.—Dark Wood or Rocky Pass in 4. Set Trees and Rocks, L. and R. Set fire U. C. Burt, Teddy and Guerrillas discovered drinking.

BURT. Fill up, boys, I've got a toast to offer. Here's to the Captain, although he wasn't with us when we captured this brandy from that old fool of a Dutchman; but, for all that, he's a trump in a fight. Come, boys, drink this standing. (*All rise and drink.*)

TEDDY. No, the Captain wasn't along, but he had a smashing

excuse. He was after a petticoat, one Maude St. Leon. and she is now imprisoned in the cabin beyant. (*Points* L. 1 E.)

BURT. Well, if the Captain wants to run away with young and pretty females, spend his time billing and cooing, and leave the lush to us, why—who cares? Not I, for one. Harry Pearson's death left the coast clear for him.

TEDDY. An' sure it's meself doesn't think he's did at all.

BURT. Didn't I see him fall into the stream after the Captain shot him?

TEDDY. Sure an' he'll be turninin' up some day like a cat wid nine lives. (*Enter Frank Duncan* R.)

BURT. Harry Pearson will never trouble us again.

FRANK D. Who says he will? Whoever dared to make that assertion lied. Fools, did I not shoot him down from the log, and watch him plunge headlong into the stream? Does not his curse ring in my ears—and when I try to sleep, do I not see him and his cursed uncle in my dreams? But no more—let me hear no more of him. I tell you once for all, he is dead—dead, I say!

BURT. For heaven's sake never mention the subject again in his presence.

FRANK D. Give me some brandy. (*Teddy fills glass.*) Fill it up. (*Puts hand on breast.*) There is something there 'twould take oceans of liquor to remove.

TEDDY. (*Aside.*) Begorra, the double murder sits hards upon his conscience. (*Enter Harker* R.)

FRANK D. What now, Harker?

HARKER. A wagon train is approaching by the turnpike, and our scouts report that it is weakly guarded.

FRANK D. Men, at once to your saddles, leave not one Northern hireling to tell the tale. Harker, conduct Maude St. Leon to this place; I wish a short conversation with her. (*Exit Harker.*) Now. Maude St. Leon, you are in my power; I swore I would possess you, and I have kept my word. Harry Pearson is dead, and I have naught to fear from any source. (*Enter Harker and Maude* L. 1 E.) Thanks, Harker, at once to the men and I will join you in a moment. (*Exit Harker* R. 1 E.) Hark you girl; time enough has elapsed since the death of your cousin for all purposes of mourning; I am going on a short expedition and you must make preparations at once, as our wedding will take place to-night.

MAUDE. Frank Duncan, I am a prisoner, torn from a loving mother's arms. You murdered my father and cousin, and as you fear heaven's wrath do not dare to carry your threat into execution.

FRANK D. Good, I like to see a little spirit in the one I love. First, one kiss, then to horse, (*Starts toward Maude.*)

MAUDE. Back! I warn you not to approach. (*Enter Harker quick* R.)

HARKER. The men are getting impatient, Captain.

FRANK D. To horse at once. (*Exit Harker* R.) I will postpone my chaste salute 'till my return, (*calling*) Teddy! Where can that Irishman be. Teddy! (*Teddy enters* R.)

TEDDY. Here I am, sur,

FRANK D. Keep a strict watch on that girl. I will hold you responsible for her safe keeping. (*Exit* R.)

TEDDY. Begorra look at the foin girl I have got to guard. (*Marches* R. to L.)

MAUDE. He has gone at last! who will aid me now?

TEDDY. Begorra, Miss, its meself will do that same thing.

MAUDE. You? why you belong to his band.

TEDDY. Yes, an' no mam. It was meself that helped your lover Harry to escape from prison.

MAUDE. Only to be murdered in cold blood.

TEDDY. Don't belave it, Miss. Though I can't explain, I have my rasons for sayin' I don't belave he was kilt at all.

MAUDE. But what reasons have you for assisting me; do you not know that if you are discovered you will pay the penalty with your life?

TEDDY. I am aware of all that; but whin I was starvin, Harry Pearson gave me mate and drink, and, Miss, Teddy O'Connor niver forgits a kindness.

MAUDE. Heaven will bless you, my friend; but is there no way to escape from here?

TEDDY. Not at present, the place is strongly guarded; but I will hasten to the Union camp an' return wid a large force.

MAUDE. Go at once. But first, have you a revolver?

TEDDY. Yis, take this, (*shows bottle,*) excuse me, ma'am, that was my spectacle case, (*produces revolver,*) take this.

MAUDE. Warn the Federal General, who is an old friend of fathers, of my danger.

TEDDY. Begorra, Miss, I'm the bye to do it. (*Exit Teddy* R. *in haste.*)

MAUDE. This shall be my protection if he fails to return in time. (*Sits down on bench or rock* L.)

SCENE II.—Wood in 2. (Enter General U. S. A., and Cololonel Franklin, R. 2 E.)

GENERAL. 'Tis strange that nothing reliable has been reported by our many scouts concerning the fate of Pearson.

COL. FRANKLIN. What do you think of the report that we was killed by Frank Duncan?

GENERAL. I hardly give it the least credence, (*looks* L.) Here comes White, whom I sent to obtain information concerning the whereabouts of Frank Duncan's band of Guerrillas. (*Enter White* L.) What brings you back so quickly?

WHITE. General, I had hardly set forth upon the expedition you sent me when I met one of Frank Duncan's men, who said he had information of importance to impart to you.

GENERAL. Where is this man?

WHITE. But a short distance from here. I will call him. Teddy! Teddy O'Connor!

GENERAL. A more villainous set than those Guerrillas never drew breath. Let me gain but a clue to their whereabouts, and they shall be blotted from the earth's surface. (*Enter Teddy* L.)

TEDDY. That's me name, an' how are yese, gintlemin?

WHITE. This is the man, General.

GENERAL. Well, sir, what do you know concerning Frank Duncan's band?

TEDDY. Sure yer honor they are encamped down on an old plantation about tin miles beyant this place. I left but a short time ago to git help to rescue a poor female woman from his clutches.

GENERAL. How many men compose his band?

TEDDY. Sure, sur, ave I was on me oath, I should say about wan hundred, sur.

GENERAL. Who is this girl or woman that is imprisoned there?

TEDDY. Her name is Maude St. Leon, sur.

GENERAL. The daughter of my old friend; can you lead us to this plantation?

TEDDY. I'm the bye that can do that same ting.

GENERAL. Do you know anything concerning Harry Pearson?

TEDDY. Sure, sur, didn't I help him to escape from Belle Isle prison.

GENERAL. You did, and where is he now? (*Enter Harry* L. *with his head bandaged.*)

HARRY. Here General, once more ready to fight against any traitor to the glorious old Stars and Stripes.

GENERAL. (*Shaking Harry's hand.*) You are just in time, we were about making up a detachment to attack Frank Duncan's Guerrillas, and rescue your cousin Maude, who is held a close prisoner. But how did you escape?

HARRY. 'Twill take but a few words to tell my story. I was imprisoned at Belle Isle for six months and nearly starved to death, when this friend (*pointing to Teddy*) furnished me with a disguise and the countersign.

TEDDY. Sure that's me.

HARRY. While in the swamps I was pursued by blood-hounds. I killed them both, and had gained a log which led across a stream, when I was discovered by Frank Duncan, who fired, the ball striking my head; stunned and faint for the loss of blood I fell into the water, but was rescued by Deitrick. I bade him mention to no one of my rescue, wishing Frank Duncan to believe me dead. But let us start at once, I yearn for the moment when I can meet him face to face. (*Enter Deitrick* L. 1 E.)

DEITRICK. ————you vas in pet.

HARRY. I was a short time ago, and whould be there still if I had obeyed your orders. But Deitrick we are making up a party to attack Frank Duncan's guerrillas.

DEITRICK. ————dot fighdin pisness.

HARRY. I am good for many encounters with the enemies of my country.

DEITRICK. ————me dwo.

GENERAL. Colonel Franklin order your men to their saddles.

and I will take command in person. (*Exit General, Staff, Harry, White and Col. Franklin,* R.)

DEITRICK. ———— Hallo, Teddy!

TEDDY. Begorra, how are yese Deitrick?

DEITRICK. ————a Union man?

TEDDY. Well I am.

DEITRICK. ————a good Union man?

TEDDY. Sure I'm as good a wan as yese.

DEITRICK. ————you dook something.

TEDDY. I'm the bye that will do that same ting.

DEITRICK. ————dook a walk. (*Exit* R.)

SCENE III.—Same as scene 1. Lights part down. (Maude discovered.)

MAUDE. Teddy not returned. I fear that he has failed in his mission, if so, then my only resource will be this revolver he so kindly gave me. Hark, I hear Frank Duncan and his men returning. I had hoped for a longer respite from his presence. (*Enter Frank Duncan and Mrs. St. Leon* R. 1 E.)

FRANK D. I have brought you a visitor, Miss Maude.

MRS. ST. L. (*Embracing Maude.*) My dear, dear daughter.

MAUDE. Mother!

FRANK D. You can retire to yonder cabin and make all the arrangements for our approaching marriage, which takes place to-night.

MAUDE. Come mother, let us be together while we can. (*Exit* L.)

FRANK D. Everything is working to my wishes; by jove though, that was a fat haul to-day. (*Enter Burt and Guerrillas* R. *with bottles.*) Well boys, as you have done a good day's work, fill up your glasses and make a merry night of it. (*Guerrillas fill glasses.*)

BURT. Here's a health, Captain, and many returns.

FRANK D. Thank you, my brave men, and in return I will invite you to my wedding.

BURT. Long live the Captain. (*Guerrillas cheer.*) When does

FRANK D. This night, in one hour. Fill up men and drink a bumper to my fair bride, Maude St. Leon. (*All drink. Enter Harker* R.)

HARKER. Captain, a large force of Union Cavalry is approaching by the main road; 'tis too late to retreat, we must meet them here.

FRANK D. Out men, fall in and fight for your lives. (*Exit Burt and Guerrillas* R. Harker, where is that Irishman, Teddy?

HARKER. I have not seen him since morning.

FRANK D. Curse him! 'tis he that has brought this Yankee horde upon us. At once to the men, have them ready to repel any attack that may be made. (*Exit Harker* R.; *Enter Maude and Mrs. St. Leon* L.)

MRS. ST. L. The avengers are on your path, do not court destruction, fly, or your blood will be upon your own head.

FRANK D. What! Frank Duncan, who fears neither man nor devil, desert his men, what can you mean?

MAUDE. Do you not fear death, with such a terrible load of guilt upon your soul?

FRANK D. I have no time to bandy words with women. Do not leave this place under any consideration. (*Exit* R. *in haste. Shots heard.*)

MAUDE. Mother, I am sure my hour of deliverance has arrived.

MRS. ST. L. We will hope for the best. (*Firing outside. Enter Harker* R., *staggers to* C., *falls.*)

HARKER. Mrs. St. Leon, I am dying—forgive me for all the pain and suffering I have caused you and yours—forgive——(*dies.*)

MRS. ST. L. May God forgive you, as I freely do.

MAUDE. Oh mother, I hope the Union army will be victorious. (*Enter Frank Duncan* R.)

FRANK D. All is lost, but Maude St. Leon, you shall be mine in death if not in life. (*Draws dagger, starts toward Maude. Shot heard. Frank Duncan staggers.*)

FRANK D. I am shot, but death shall still wed us. (*Enter Deitrick* R. *with gun, strikes him down. Duncan falls.*)

DEITRICK. ————Misdur Guerriller? (*Enter Harry, White, General U. S. A., Col. Franklin and Officers* R.)

MAUDE. Harry, are you alive and safe?

HARRY.   Yes, my dear Maude.   Aunt, have you no word for me?

MRS. ST. L.   We welcome you as from the grave.

FRANK D.   (*Rising up painfully.*)   Curse you, Harry Pearson, can you not stay in your grave; and you, old man, go back from whence you came; do not stare at me with those glassy eyes. Back—back I——(*falls dead.*)

DEITRICK.   ————done dot.

MAUDE.   Misguided man, he is dead; and Harry, I am thankful that you did not stain your hands with his blood.

HARRY.   Let us try to forgive him for his many injuries to all. He is dead, and "The Avenger's" mission is ended.

(*Tableau—Curtain.*)

This Book must be returned to the Manager, or paid for.

[**Price, Twenty-Five Cents.**]

www.ingramcontent.com/pod-product-compliance
Lightning Source LLC
Chambersburg PA
CBHW061237260626
47172CB00003B/894